Bedtime for Porcupine

Written by Michèle Dufresne • Illustrated by Sterling Lamet

PIONEER VALLEY EDUCATIONAL PRESS, INC.

Porcupine was playing
hide and seek
with Squirrel and Rabbit.
"Time for bed," called his mother.

"It's not dark yet," said Porcupine.

"It will be dark very soon,"
said his mother.
"Come inside
and get ready for bed."

Porcupine washed
his hands and face.
Then he brushed his teeth.

"Get into bed,"
said Mother Porcupine.

"It's not dark yet!" said Porcupine.

"It will be dark very soon,"
said his mother.

"Will you read me a story?"
Porcupine asked his mother.

Mother Porcupine read Porcupine
a story about winter in the forest.
"Now go to sleep,"
said his mother.

"It's not dark yet!" said Porcupine.

"It will be dark very soon,"
said Mother Porcupine.

"Will you read me another story?"
Porcupine asked.

"All right. One more story,"
said his mother.
She read Porcupine a story
about spring in the forest.

"Now go to sleep,"
said Mother Porcupine.

"It's not dark yet!" said Porcupine.

Mother Porcupine looked at her watch. "It will be dark very, very soon," she said.

"Will you read me another story?" asked Porcupine.

"All right. One more story," said his mother.
She read Porcupine a story about summer in the forest.

Mother Porcupine tucked Porcupine into bed.

"I have read three stories," she told him.
"Now you must go to sleep!"
She turned off the light.

"But I can't go to sleep,"
said Porcupine.
"I'm afraid of the dark!"